MISSI

Flame

Have you seen this kitten?

Flame is a magic kitten of royal blood, missing from his own world.
His uncle, Ebony, is very keen that he is found quickly.
Flame may be hard to spot as he often appears in a
variety of fluffy kitten colours but you can recognize him
by his big emerald eyes and whiskers that crackle with magic!

He is believed to be looking for a young friend to take care of him.

Could it be you?

If you find this very special kitten please let Ebony,
ruler of the Lion Throne, know.

Sue Bentley's books for children often include animals or fairies. She lives in Northampton and enjoys reading, going to the cinema, and sitting watching the frogs and newts in her garden pond. If she hadn't been a writer she would probably have been a skydiver or a brain surgeon. The main reason she writes is that she can drink pots and pots of tea while she's typing. She has met and owned many cats and each one has brought a special sort of magic to her life.

Magic Kitten

Summer Spell

SUE BENTLEY

Illustrated by Angela Swan

PUFFIN

Bradley — my lovely laid-back blue boy

PUFFIN BOOKS

Published by the Penguin Group
Penguin Books Ltd, 80 Strand, London WC2R ORL, England
Penguin Group (USA) Inc., 375 Hudson Street, New York, New York 10014, USA
Penguin Group (Canada), 90 Eglinton Avenue East, Suite 700, Toronto, Ontario,
Canada M4P 2Y3 (a division of Pearson Penguin Canada Inc.)
Penguin Ireland, 25 St Stephen's Green, Dublin 2, Ireland
(a division of Penguin Books Ltd)
Penguin Group (Australia), 250 Camberwell Road, Camberwell, Victoria 3124,
Australia (a division of Pearson Australia Group Pty Ltd)
Penguin Books India Pvt Ltd, 11 Community Centre,
Panchsheel Park, New Delhi – 110 017, India
Penguin Group (NZ), cnr Airborne and Rosedale Roads, Albany, Auckland 1310,
New Zealand (a division of Pearson New Zealand Ltd)
Penguin Books (South Africa) (Pty) Ltd, 24 Sturdee Avenue,
Rosebank, Johannesburg 2196, South Africa

Penguin Books Ltd, Registered Offices: 80 Strand, London WC2R ORL, England

penguin.com

First published 2006
8

Text copyright © Sue Bentley, 2006
Illustrations copyright © Angela Swan, 2006
All rights reserved

The moral right of the author and illustrator has been asserted

Set in Bembo by Palimpsest Book Production Limited,
Grangemouth, Stirlingshire
Made and printed in England by Clays Ltd, St Ives plc

British Library Cataloguing in Publication Data
A CIP catalogue record for this book is available from the British Library

ISBN-13: 978-0-141-32014-4

Prologue

There was a flash of bright white light and a shower of silver sparkles. Where the young white lion had stood, now crouched a tiny, fluffy, marmalade kitten. Overhead, grey clouds skidded across a huge red moon.

Suddenly an old grey lion ran up to the little kitten and bowed his head. 'Prince Flame! Hurry! Your Uncle

Ebony comes! If he finds you, he will kill you. You must use this disguise and hide until your powers grow stronger.'

'Cirrus! Save yourself,' Flame mewed, his emerald eyes flashing. 'I will face him.'

'Please, Flame. You must hide,' Cirrus urged.

Flame shivered. 'Hide where? My kingdom is taken. Uncle's spies are everywhere . . .'

Cirrus laid a paw on the young prince's little marmalade head. 'Go far away. Grow strong and wise. Return then, to claim the Lion Throne and rid the land from this terrible evil.'

Something moved on the lower slopes. Flame gasped as an enormous adult lion surged upwards in great, muscular bounds that ate up the wet grass. His terrifying teeth were bared.

Silver sparks ignited in Flame's fur and the kitten mewed as he felt the power building inside him.

Just as the older lion leapt on to a flat rock and gathered himself for a final spring, there was a bright blue flash. Flame heard a roar of rage, then felt himself falling. Falling . . .

Chapter
* ONE *

Lisa Morgan gave a sigh as the train drew to a halt. Long Brackby station had no waiting room. There was just a wooden platform and some steps that led down to the road. All around there was miles of open countryside.

'Great, I'm being dumped in the middle of nowhere,' she grumbled. 'Thanks a lot, Mum and Dad!'

Her parents had gone to America on business. But Lisa was going to stay with her Aunt Rose, who she hadn't seen since she was a baby.

Lisa scanned the platform. She saw a woman with plaits and flowing clothes hurrying towards her. Her heart sank. Aunt Rose was an old hippie!

I bet she has weird ideas about food, Lisa thought glumly. She imagined being force-fed beans, lettuce and raw carrots. She pictured herself looking all limp and pale. Wouldn't that just serve her parents right?

The hippie woman smiled. She dashed straight past Lisa and jumped on the train.

'Phew!' Lisa breathed, feeling relieved but a bit disappointed. She had quite liked the idea of making her parents feel guilty for not taking her with them.

Just then a voice called out, 'Hi, Lisa! I'm over here!'

A slim woman with wavy brown hair was climbing the platform steps. She wore jeans and a yellow T-shirt. She waved at Lisa.

Lisa waved back.

'Sorry I'm a bit late.' Rose gathered Lisa up and gave her a big hug. She then held Lisa at arm's length and studied her. 'Gosh, aren't you tall for ten years old?'

'Everyone says that,' Lisa murmured. 'Dad says I take after him.'

'I expect you're right.' Rose's smile was warm. It made her eyes twinkle. 'It's so lovely to have you for the school holidays. We can really get to know each other.'

Lisa felt cheered by Rose's warm welcome. But she wasn't ready to let go of her bad mood. 'I didn't want to come here. Mum forced me to stay with you.'

Rose looked amused. She picked up

Lisa's suitcase. 'Well — I'd better make sure you enjoy yourself then. Long Brackby may not compare with America, but it has a lot to offer. Come on. Let's go home. The car's this way.'

Lisa followed her aunt down the steps. The car park was empty. 'Has someone stolen your car?' she asked worriedly.

'Oh, no. Matilda's over there.' Rose pointed across a wide field. 'She conked out on me, I'm afraid. That's why I was late.'

Lisa craned her neck. She could just see the rounded top of a red car above a hedge. It looked about a hundred miles away!

Rose grinned at Lisa's expression. 'It's

only a short walk. I expect you could do with stretching your legs after two hours on the train.' She opened a big wooden gate and stepped into the field.

Lisa hung back nervously. There were lots of enormous black and white cows in the field. 'Won't they chase us?' she asked.

'Not if we don't chase them,' Rose joked. 'Just follow me. You'll be fine.' She closed the gate behind them and set off.

After a couple of metres Rose stopped suddenly. 'Oh, look, how pretty. That's ragged robin . . .' She pointed to a clump of pink wild flowers.

'Oh.' Lisa almost bumped into her aunt. She was keeping a wary eye on the cows. One of them, which looked about the size of a bus, was staring hard at her. She was sure it was going to charge at any moment. Rose set off again. 'Lisa, you'd better watch out for the . . .' she began.

Lisa's foot sank right into something soft and smelly. She skidded and almost slipped over. 'Ugh! How gross is that!'

'. . . cowpats,' Rose finished.

'My trainers!' Lisa wailed. 'They're ruined.'

Rose's mouth twitched. 'Oh, well, it's only a bit of old poo. We can hose it off when we get home. Good thing you didn't slip over and sit in it!'

Lisa scowled at Rose. 'Ha, ha,' she muttered crossly.

Peering down at her trainer, Lisa hopped about on one foot, trying to wipe the sole clean on the grass. When she looked up again, she saw that Rose was almost at the other end of the field.

'Wait for me!' she shouted in panic. She zoomed across the field and shot through the gate. There was no way

she going to be left behind with the
cows, to be trampled into a human
pancake!

Rose walked along the grass verge
until she came to her car. 'Here we
are. Say hello to Matilda.'

Rose's VW Beetle was painted
black and tomato red. It looked
like a giant, rather battered
ladybird.

'Oh − my − goodness,' Lisa
mouthed silently. 'Will that old thing
start?'

'*She*, please,' Rose corrected,
'Matilda always starts after a rest. She
opened the bonnet, which Lisa saw
was actually the boot, and put
Lisa's suitcase inside. When they were
both seated, Rose gunned the

engine. 'Hurrah! First time!' she cried.

Despite herself, Lisa smiled.

A couple of minutes later, they drew up outside a neat thatched cottage. White roses scrambled all over the honey-coloured stone walls.

'Leave your trainers on the front step. You can clean them later,' Rose said. 'I expect you'd like a cold drink.'

'Yes, please.' Lisa followed her aunt through to the kitchen. A big iron kettle sat on top of Rose's cooker. There was also a deep sink and a wooden dresser, but no dishwasher, toaster or microwave.

'Now, what can I get you?' asked Rose.

'A Coke, please,' Lisa said.

Rose frowned. 'I'm afraid I've only got lemonade. It's home-made. Would you like to try it?'

Lisa wrinkled her nose, but she was dying of thirst so she accepted a glass. She took a tiny sip. It wasn't as bad as she'd expected.

'Come on. I'll give you the grand tour.' Rose led the way into a room filled with afternoon sunshine.

Lisa saw a sofa with big patchwork cushions and lots of bookcases. 'Through there is my workroom.' Rose pointed towards an open door.

Lisa peered inside. There were shelves piled with folded material, and glass jars crammed with colourful beads and buttons. 'I thought Mum said you were an artist.'

Rose chuckled. 'I'm a textile artist. I make patchwork quilts and wall hangings.'

'Oh,' Lisa said. That sounded really boring. 'What's upstairs?'

Rose explained that there were two bedrooms. One was hers and Lisa would be using the other.

'It's a bit small, isn't it?' Lisa said. She was sure Rose's entire cottage would fit into the sitting room of her parents' flat in London.

'I prefer to think of it as cosy,' said Rose with a smile. 'It suits me just fine. Why don't we sit down and finish our drinks before I show you your room?'

'OK,' Lisa shrugged. She plonked herself down on Rose's squishy sofa.

Something didn't seem quite right with the room. Then, with a shock, she realized why. 'You haven't got a TV!'

'Oh, I don't bother with watching the box. I always have so much to do,' Rose said.

Lisa was speechless. She didn't know *anyone* who didn't have a TV.

Rose took one look at Lisa's glum face. She chuckled. 'I've an old set in the cupboard. I'll get it for you, if you like.'

Lisa shrugged. 'I don't mind.'

Five minutes later Rose came in carrying a small black and white TV. 'Here you go.'

Lisa just stared. 'It's only got four channels!'

Rose frowned. 'How many should it have?'

'I don't know. But ours at home has at least thirty.'

'Really?' Rose looked astonished. 'However do they fill that many channels? Well, if you don't want it . . .'

'No, I do. I do!' Lisa decided quickly.

She watched as Rose set about plugging in the TV. No microwave and a TV that should be in a museum. This holiday was going to be a nightmare.

Chapter
TWO

As Lisa finished stuffing her clothes into a drawer, her aunt called up the stairs.

'Lisa! Why don't you have a look round outside while I'm cooking supper? There's something that might interest you in the barn.'

Lisa padded downstairs in her socks. Rose was in the kitchen by the back door. She gave Lisa some green wellington boots. 'You can borrow these.'

Lisa rolled her eyes. 'Oh, good!' she murmured.

Rose chuckled. 'They might not be the height of fashion, but they'll keep your feet clean!'

Rose's garden had a long narrow lawn and a big vegetable plot. The old barn was right at the bottom. Lisa wandered down to it. She hoped the barn wasn't dark and creepy and full of horrible spiders.

Just as she opened the door there was a bright silver flash. Lisa thought she saw a large white shape out of the corner of her eye. She turned her head, but saw only a pile of old newspapers.

She pushed the door wide open and
poked her head in. A warm, slightly
musty, smell greeted her. It was
somehow familiar. Lisa went right
inside. She could see rows of cages
and pens. Now she recognized that
smell. It was just like inside a pet
shop.

'Look at all these animals! This is
great!' There were rabbits, guinea pigs

and even some hedgehogs. 'Aunt Rose must be into animal rescue.'

Sacks of animal food were stored on a bench. Lisa noticed a glow coming from one of the food sacks. 'That's strange.' She went over to investigate.

'Oh!' She gazed in amazement.

A fluffy marmalade-coloured kitten was curled up on one of the sacks. Its silky coat looked as soft as thistledown. Silver sparkles glittered in the air around it and its whiskers crackled like electricity.

Lisa stared and stared at the kitten. It looked so real. Was it some kind of new toy? No cat in the world sparkled like that.

Suddenly the kitten's eyes shot open. It took one look at Lisa and hurtled into the air on stiff little legs.

'Miaow! Monster!' it cried fearfully.

'Argh!' Lisa yelled in shock. Did this kitten really just speak?

Lisa took a step back, fell over her own feet and landed on her bottom in the straw.

The kitten gazed at her with glowing emerald eyes. Its fur all stood on end. Silver sparkles crackled all round it. 'What are you?' it demanded in a velvety miaow.

'I'm a girl,' Lisa stammered in complete shock. 'What are you?'

But the kitten didn't seem to hear her. 'A girl?' it repeated to itself. 'Strange. You have two legs. No tail or whiskers.'

'Of course I haven't! I'm not a cat!' Lisa said. She rose to her feet slowly, so that the amazing kitten wouldn't run away. 'My name's Lisa Morgan.'

'Lisa,' the kitten mewed, looking up at her. It seemed strangely unafraid of her, despite how tiny it was. 'Where is this place, Lisa?'

'It's a village called Long Brackby,' she replied. 'My Aunt Rose lives here. I'm staying with her for the holidays. What are you doing here? Who are you? *What* are you?'

'I am Prince Flame,' replied the kitten, sitting up very straight. 'Heir to the Lion Throne.'

'Wow! Really?' Lisa was having trouble taking everything in. A royal cat. A magic, talking cat. Here in her aunt's barn! Lisa thought for a moment. She was confused. 'Did you say *Lion* Throne? But you're only a kit—' She was suddenly interrupted as Flame pricked up his ears.

'What is that big noise?'

Lisa heard a car go by on the road outside. 'Just a car. It's OK. It won't hurt you.' She had a sudden thought. 'Are you hungry? Aunt Rose must have loads of cat food. I can get you some if you like.'

Lisa saw Flame's eyes light up at the thought of food. 'You are kind, Lisa. This is a safe place.'

He leapt forward. There was a bright blue flash and a crackle of silver sparks.

'Oh!' Lisa was blinded for a second. When her sight cleared, she saw that in Flame's place stood a young, regal, white lion. Then just as suddenly as it had appeared, Flame returned as the fluffy marmalade kitten.

'Flame? Was that you?' she gasped. 'You really are a lion prince!'

Flame blinked up at her with wide, emerald-green eyes. 'I am in danger. I must hide. Will you keep me safe?' he asked in a tiny mew.

Lisa's heart melted. Flame was impressive as a royal lion. Disguised as a kitten he was adorable. 'Oh, of course I will!' Picking him up, she gently stroked the top of his head. Then she paused for a moment. 'But what are you hiding from?'

Flame placed his tiny paws on Lisa's chest and looked up at her. 'My uncle wants my throne. His spies seek me here. He wants – he wants to kill me.'

'Well, they'll have to fight me first!' Lisa said fiercely. 'I'll look after you, Flame,' she promised. 'You'll be my secret. My secret magic kitten. Although I don't know what I'm going to tell Aunt Rose. She's going to notice you if you live here.'

'Notice who?' asked a voice at her side. 'Who are you talking to, Lisa?'

Lisa almost jumped out of her skin. She hadn't heard Aunt Rose come into the barn.

Chapter
* THREE *

'I found Flame asleep on a feed sack.
Please can I keep him?' Lisa asked,
stroking Flame's tiny ears.

'Flame? I see you've already given
him a name.' Rose stroked the kitten's
soft marmalade fur. 'He's beautiful all
right. But we should find out where he
lives. He's not one of the rescued
animals, you know.'

'He hasn't got a home or he wouldn't
be sleeping in a barn, would he?' Lisa
reasoned. She had promised Flame she
would take care of him and there was *no
way* she was letting him down. 'If you let
Flame live here, I'll do everything for
him. I'll buy his food out of my pocket
money. He can sleep in my bedroom.
And . . . and . . . I'll clean out pongy
animal cages and everything!'

Rose laughed. 'You're determined to keep him, aren't you?'

'Completely!' Lisa said spiritedly. 'So — can he stay?'

'You'd best give him to me then,' Rose said. 'I'll check him for fleas and ticks before he comes into the house.'

'Brilliant! You can stay here. We're going to be the best of friends,' Lisa whispered, giving Flame a swift hug before handing him to her aunt.

'Hello there, you sweet thing.' Rose ran expert fingers through Flame's soft coat. 'No flea dirt showing, so far.' She then turned him over and searched the paler fur on his fat, round tummy. 'Good, none there either.'

Flame wriggled and mewed in protest.

Lisa had to bite back a grin. She suspected this was the first time a lion prince had been searched for fleas!

Rose finished her examination. 'He's clean and in very good condition. I expect he's hungry. You'll find food and a feeding dish on that shelf.'

'Thanks, Aunt Rose! You're wonderful!' Lisa hugged her aunt on impulse.

Rose gave her a pleased smile. 'Anyone would think you'd never had a pet!'

'I haven't. Mum says it isn't fair to have animals in a town flat.' Lisa opened a tin, forked food into a dish and set it on the floor.

Flame purred loudly as he munched the cat food.

'Well, I agree with your mum about pets,' Rose said seriously. 'Don't get too attached to Flame. You'll have a tough decision to make when you go back to London.'

Lisa knew that Rose was right. But it was too late. She had promised Flame she would look after him, and this magic kitten was the one good thing that had happened since her parents had left her here. She didn't want to give him up!

Flame licked his lips when he'd finished the food. He came and rubbed his body against Lisa's legs. She bent down to stroke him and he mewed softly, so only she heard him.

'I am safe with you. Thank you, Lisa.'

Rose dug a scoop into a sack of rabbit food. 'Just time to feed this lot before supper.'

'I'll help.' This wasn't exactly Lisa's idea of fun but she was determined to show that she meant to keep her promise and make certain that Flame could stay.

For the next half-hour she refilled

water bottles, chopped vegetables and replaced soiled straw.

Flame settled down, tucked his paws beneath his body and dozed.

'Thanks, love,' Rose said later, as she and Lisa washed their hands. 'I bet you're ready to eat. I know I am.'

Lisa scooped up the sleepy kitten and followed Rose back to the cottage. Rose gave her an old blanket and Lisa spread it on the sofa. Flame jumped straight up and began pedalling it into a soft nest with his front paws.

A few minutes later, Rose brought heaped plates of food to the table.

'Er . . . thanks.' Lisa poked the food with her knife. It was shepherd's pie with a lot of fresh green stuff next to it.

'That's called salad. We eat a lot in
the country. It's the law!' Rose kept a
straight face.

'I get the message,' Lisa said with a
grin. The pie was delicious and she
even ate some of the salad. Afterwards,
Lisa went to sit near Flame on the
sofa. 'Thanks, Aunt Rose. I think I'll
curl up with Flame and watch TV
now.'

'Do you mind doing that later?' Rose said. 'House rules are — I cook, you wash up. OK?'

'Oh, right.' Lisa felt herself blush. She jumped up and collected the dishes. Wasn't there even a dishwasher here?

In the kitchen, Lisa filled the sink with hot water and squirted washing-up liquid over the pots and pans. As she began scrubbing them clean, suds foamed up past her elbows. 'Oo-er,' she said worriedly, as more suds waterfalled on to the kitchen floor and slopped round her feet. 'I think I overdid it! What a mess. Aunt Rose is going to kill me!'

'May I help?' came a tiny voice from the kitchen floor.

She turned to see that Flame stood

behind her. His marmalade fur was fizzing with huge silver sparkles, his whiskers crackled and his eyes glowed like emerald coals. Lisa felt a hot prickling sensation down her spine.

Something was about to happen!

Chapter
* FOUR *

Flame leapt up into the air like a silver fireball and landed on the draining board. Sparks crackled from the tips of his ears.

He waved his front paws and plates, spoons, forks, knives and pans all dunked themselves in the suds. One by one, they jumped into the air and spun themselves dry.

Lisa's eyes widened. 'Wow! This is *so* cool!'

Cupboard doors flew open and clean plates stacked themselves on the shelves. Drawers opened, so that forks, knives and spoons could zoom inside.

Lisa watched the suds drain away. The dishcloth did a little dance as it

wiped the sink clean. Another cloth
shimmied across the kitchen floor.
'Look at them go!' She clapped her
hands with delight.

'Lisa? Are you all right? There's a lot
of noise in there,' Rose called from the
sitting room.

'Oh, no!' Lisa's hand flew to her
mouth. She waved frantically at Flame.
'Quick. Stop doing whatever you're
doing!' she hissed. 'I'm fine. Almost
finished!' she called to her aunt, in
what she hoped was a normal voice.

Crash! Cupboard doors closed. Bang!
Drawers slammed shut. Rattle! Cutlery
settled into place.

Seconds later, Rose popped her head
round the kitchen door. 'What *is* going
on out here?'

Flame sat on the floor, looking just like a normal marmalade kitten. Phew! Lisa let out her breath and gave her aunt a rather shaky smile. That was a near thing!

'I'm really impressed. The whole kitchen's spotless. Well done,' Rose said admiringly.

'Oh, it was nothing,' Lisa said, shining the back of her nails on her T-shirt.

She winked at Flame, who gave a mischievous 'miaow'.

A big bubble of laughter lodged in Lisa's chest. With Flame around, she reckoned this holiday might not be so bad after all.

The following morning, Lisa woke early. She lay with her eyes closed, listening for the sound of traffic and taxi horns hooting in impatience. But only birdsong drifted in on the fresh breeze from the open window. Lisa opened her eyes as she remembered where she was.

Aunt Rose's cottage in Long Brackby. And yesterday she had found a magic kitten in the barn! He was curled up asleep in the crook of her arm.

Flame purred softly in his sleep. As Lisa stroked him gently, Flame stretched and yawned, showing his little pink tongue and sharp white teeth. Silver sparks glittered in his fur.

'I slept well, thank you,' he purred happily.

'Me too,' Lisa said as Flame rubbed his head under her chin. 'That tickles!' she said with a grin. She pulled herself up out of bed and went in search of the bathroom as Flame made himself comfy on her pillow and waited.

Rose was already in the kitchen when Lisa came down. Lisa fed Flame before she ate her breakfast and then helped Rose clear up, smiling as she remembered how the dishes had got cleaned yesterday!

'Do you fancy cycling to the village
store?' Rose asked. 'We need milk,
bread and eggs, but I've got heaps of
sewing to do,' she explained. 'You could
use my bike. It would help me out and
would give you a chance to explore.'

'Sounds great,' Lisa said. Having
Flame along would make even boring
old shopping fun!

Rose fetched her bike. It had a deep basket on the front. Lisa lined it with Flame's blanket and then lifted him in. 'There. It's just right for you!'

Flame purred softly in agreement.

Rose laughed. 'You know, I think that kitten understands every word you say!'

She came round to the front of the cottage to give Lisa directions to the village shops. 'Go up Berry Road to the crossroads and turn right. You'll see the White Hart Inn. The shops are just a bit farther on. You can't miss them.'

Rose's red and black VW Beetle was parked by the gate. 'Hi, Matilda!' Lisa called as she cycled past. 'See you later, Aunt Rose!'

The honey scent of hawthorn filled

the lane. Skylarks circled overhead, drifting on the warm air. Flame had his nose in the air, sniffing the delicious country smells.

'Now – we turn here,' Lisa reminded herself.

Berry Road was narrow and lined with trees. Lisa began to slow down as she approached a sharp bend.

Suddenly a brown and white pony came hurtling towards her. Lisa caught a glimpse of the rider pulling at the reins. The pony's ears were flat against its head. It snorted loudly, flaring its nostrils.

'Watch out!' shouted the rider. 'I can't stop him!'

Lisa squeezed the brakes hard so that pebbles sprayed the grass verge. Flame dug his claws into the basket to brace himself.

But it was too late. They were going to crash!

Chapter
FIVE

Lisa's bike screeched along the road
into the pony. The brakes locked and
she was launched into the air. Just as
she prepared herself for a very painful
landing there was a silver flash and she
landed softly on to what felt like a very
soft pillow.

'Oh!' she cried in surprise. She
pushed herself shakily to her feet and

looked down, but there was just the grass verge beneath her. That was a near thing. Flame must have used his magic to save her! But where was he?

Lisa looked round in panic. In the road she saw the pony was snorting with pain and fear. His rider was trying to calm him down. Aunt Rose's bike lay on its side in the road, the pedals still going round. Flame's crumpled blanket was lying beside it.

Lisa's heart lurched. 'Oh, no! Flame!'

But Flame was sitting in the gutter, calmly washing his face. He gave a pleased little miaow as she bent down to stroke him.

'Oh, thank goodness you're OK!' Lisa said.

'Yeah? Well, Fly's not. And it's all your fault!' shouted the boy who'd been riding the pony. 'Why don't you look where you're going?'

Stung, Lisa glared at him. The boy looked about twelve. He had dark-brown hair and bright-blue eyes. 'You were on the wrong side of the road!' she protested angrily, picking up her bike.

But the boy ignored her. 'Whoa, there. Calm down, Fly!' he soothed. The pony rolled his eyes and kept lifting one back leg. 'Oh, great. Now he's lame! Dad's going to kill me. We haven't got any money for vets' bills.'

Lisa felt sorry for the pony, but she
was still furious with its owner. 'You
should be more careful how you ride
him then! Look at my aunt's bike. The
front wheel's all buckled!'

Flame finished washing himself. He
padded over to Fly. Lisa started forward
in alarm. Did Flame realize what
danger he was in?

'Get that kitten out of the way. Fly's dead wary of other animals,' the boy warned.

Flame stopped right beneath Fly. He looked straight up at the pony, his emerald eyes sparkling. Fly shifted sideways and gave a nervous blow. Then he dipped his head. Flame purred loudly, closing his eyes with pleasure as Fly snuffled warm breath into his fur.

The boy scratched his head. 'Will you look at that? Fly's really taken to that kitten.' He ran a hand down his pony's sore leg. 'And his leg seems better now. How did that happen?'

Lisa smiled inwardly as she bent down and picked Flame up. 'Thanks for saving me. And making Fly's leg better,' she whispered.

'I am glad to help.' Flame licked her chin with his tiny pink tongue.

Lisa straightened up. 'Oh, well, he can't have been that hurt in the first place,' she said, trying not to laugh at the boy's confusion.

The boy scowled at her. 'Whatever,' he said. 'Come on, Fly. Let's get going.'

'Hey! What about the bike? I can't ride it like that,' Lisa said with dismay.

'Tough!' The boy grinned cheekily.

Lisa was fuming. She opened her mouth to reply just as a policeman came round the corner.

The boy groaned. 'Oh, great. It's Mike Sanders. He chucked me off the green for playing football last week.' He threw a pleading glance at Lisa. 'OK, I *was* on the wrong side of the road. I couldn't help it. Some flapping washing startled Fly and he bolted.'

Lisa folded her arms. 'So?' she said.

The boy hesitated. 'I'll make a deal with you. You keep quiet about me and Fly and I'll fix your bent wheel.'

Lisa grinned. 'Done! I'm Lisa. Lisa
Morgan.' She held out her hand. 'And
this is Flame.'

'John Wood,' said the boy. He spat in
his palm before he shook hands with
Lisa, and gave Flame a pat on the head.

The policeman had reached them by
now. Mike Sanders had fair curly hair
and a pleasant face. He took in the
bike with its bent wheel and gave John
a stern look. 'Hmm. What have you
been up to now?'

John looked down at the road and
shuffled his feet. 'Nothing,' he muttered.

Lisa took a step forward. 'It's a good
thing John came along,' she said
quickly. 'That's my Aunt Rose's bike.
The wheel buckled when I fell off.
John's offered to mend it for me.'

'Has he?' Mike Sanders looked surprised. 'Good for you, John. That should keep you out of trouble for five minutes.' After checking that Lisa wasn't hurt, he went on his way.

'Phew, that was close,' said John. He took hold of Fly's reins. 'Let's go. I live just over there.'

'Don't say "thanks" for covering for me, will you?' Lisa said.

John laughed. His blue eyes sparkled. 'OK, I won't!'

Lisa couldn't help laughing back. 'Come on, Flame.' She lifted him into the basket and wheeled the bike along in a wobbly line. John walked ahead, leading Fly.

'Down here,' John said, heading down a narrow track that branched off Berry Road.

Brambles, clustered with pink-tinged blossom, rambled through the hedgerows. Peacock butterflies fluttered around clumps of nettles near a fence. Lisa paused for a moment as she looked at a large field filled with caravans beyond an open gate.

John turned round. 'Well, are you coming or what?'

Flame gave a happy miaow. And Lisa pushed him and the wobbly bike through the gate.

Chapter
★ SIX ★

The oldest lady Lisa had ever seen came out of an old-fashioned caravan with fancy carving and red and yellow wheels. She waved at John and beckoned for him to come over.

'That's my great-grandma,' John told Lisa. 'Come and meet her.'

Lisa lifted Flame out of the basket and then laid the bike on its side in

the grass. Flame scampered straight up
the caravan's sloping wooden steps and
began rubbing himself against the old
lady's long skirts.

'He's called Flame,' Lisa told her.

John had tied up Fly before climbing
the steps. He gave his gran a kiss on
her cheek. 'Hi, Gran! All right?'

The old lady's bright eyes crinkled in
a smile. 'Fine. Come on inside and
bring your new friends. The kettle's
on,' she said as she leaned down to
stroke Flame. 'I bet you'd like a saucer
of milk, wouldn't you?'

Flame mewed eagerly.

Once inside the tiny living space, Lisa
glanced round. Shiny pots and pans
hung on hooks above a tiny stove,
which made the room baking hot.

There was a wonderful smell of
woodsmoke and lavender polish.

Flame lapped at his milk. He seemed
perfectly at home.

John came and sat near his gran.
'Gran, this is Lisa. She's staying with
her aunt in the village. Lisa, meet
Violet Wood – she's head of our
family. Even my dad's a bit afraid of
her. But I reckon her bark's a lot worse
than her bite!'

Violet gave a gap-toothed grin. 'Here!
Don't give away all me secrets!' Round
her shoulders there was a black fringed
shawl with pink roses on it. Big gold
hoops glittered in her ears.

'I like your caravan,' Lisa said politely
as Violet made tea.

'It's me wagon,' Violet corrected. 'A

true Romany don't call their home a caravan.'

'Sorry,' Lisa said.

Violet fixed her with a gaze as bright and shiny as a robin's. 'What you got to be sorry about?'

'Er . . . Nothing,' Lisa murmured.

'No cause to say you're sorry then!' Violet crowed.

John chuckled. 'Stop teasing, Gran. Lisa's all right. She put a word in for me with Mike Sanders.'

Violet poured strong tea into china cups. 'Sanders ain't a bad sort. It's that Robert Higgins you got to watch out for. He's been here again, accusing our men of taking deer. I told him I know everything that goes on round here and there's been no poaching. But he wouldn't have it. He as much as called me a liar to my face!' She sniffed indignantly.

'Who's Robert Higgins?' Lisa asked John.

'Higgins runs the estate for his Lordship,' John explained. 'That bit of forest at the back of your aunt's cottage is part of it.'

'You stay out of his way, John, you hear? He's a nasty piece of work,' Violet warned him.

'Yes, Gran.' John was serious for a moment and then he turned to Lisa. 'Gran used to travel all over the country in this wagon. She's not keen on being here on the official travellers' site.'

'I miss the open road too much.' Violet's beady eyes brightened. 'There was this one time when we was *aitched* up for the night by a river . . .'

'That means camped,' John explained, smiling at Lisa.

Violet told them about the old days, when a pony drew her wagon through the country lanes. 'All the families would meet up with their relatives at horse fairs. There would be dozens of Woods, Smiths, Lees and a hundred other names. Oh, it was grand. In late summer, we'd all travel down to Kent for the hop-picking.'

Lisa listened in fascination. A look of contentment settled on Violet's face as she stroked Flame's soft coat.

Violet saw Lisa watching closely and said, 'Flame's a grand kitten, ain't he?' She closed one eye in a broad wink. 'He's just magic.'

Lisa's eyes widened in shock. *She knows!* she thought. *Violet knows about Flame!*

'Well, Gran. I've got to get my tools to mend Lisa's bike,' John said, apparently not noticing anything. 'Thanks for the tea and stories.'

'You can bring Lisa and Flame to
see me again.' Violet came down the
wagon steps to wave goodbye. She
stood with Lisa as John walked
across to a modern, chrome-trimmed
trailer.

'Keep this special one safe,' Violet
said softly to Lisa as she stroked the top
of Flame's head. 'He'll not be with you
long.'

Lisa gathered Flame in her embrace. She felt a sharp pang at the thought of not having him around. 'I don't want him to leave, ever,' she said, her voice quivering.

Violet's eyes sparkled kindly. She patted Lisa's arm. 'I know. But his destiny is far from here. When the call comes, he must go. Be thankful that he chose you for his special friend.'

Lisa hugged Flame's furry little body close. He purred and licked her chin. She had a lump in her throat. 'I am. If I look after him really well, maybe he'll decide to stay here.'

A wise but sad look crossed Violet's face. 'Maybe,' she murmured.

★

'All finished,' John said, moving the bike back and forth. 'Good as new!'

He lifted Flame into the basket as Lisa got on the bike. 'Thanks. Aunt Rose won't notice a thing. Well – bye for now,' she said and cycled towards the site gate.

'I'm going fishing tomorrow,' John called after her. 'Want to come?'

Lisa had never been fishing, but she thought it might be better than doing nothing at her aunt's cottage. 'OK. Where shall we meet?' she shouted.

'Outside the White Hart Inn near the crossroads. Nine a.m.?'

'See you there!' Lisa waved as she turned into the lane.

The sun was low and elder trees threw long shadows across the road. 'That was quite an adventure, wasn't it?' she said to Flame.

Flame mewed agreement. He curled his front paws over the basket's rim and peered ahead, ears pricked up and fur sparkling.

At the top of the lane, Lisa paused. 'Now. Do we go right or left?'

Suddenly a dark-blue van pulled up, hooting loudly. Lisa jumped with fright. The van's broken wing mirror was only centimetres away. With a screech of tyres, the van sped off.

'Some people have no manners!' Lisa fumed, turning into Berry Road.

As she cycled towards her aunt's cottage, a niggling worry crept into her mind. It felt like she had forgotten something.

Aunt Rose's shopping!

'Oh, no!' she breathed. 'Maybe we've still got time to go to the shops.'

'We are too late.' Flame pointed a paw at the red and black VW Beetle, which was coming towards them.

Matilda drew to a halt. Lisa's aunt leaned out of the window, a furious look on her face. 'I want a word with you, young lady!' she said.

Lisa's spirits sank. 'Uh-oh,' she whispered to Flame.

Chapter
* SEVEN *

Lisa dragged her feet as she
followed her aunt into the cottage.
There was no way she could avoid a
lecture. Flame padded in behind
them.

Rose's cheeks were flushed with
anger. 'You've been gone for hours,
Lisa. I've been frantic, driving around
looking for you.'

73

'I didn't realize how late it was,' Lisa murmured, wondering what all the fuss was about. She was back now, wasn't she?

'You should have come back and told me where you were going,' Rose snapped. 'You know that I'm responsible for you while you're here. I thought you were more grown up than this.'

Lisa felt an uncomfortable twinge of guilt. 'I'm sorry, Aunt Rose. I didn't think.' She told her aunt all about almost crashing into John on Fly, then going to the travellers' site and having tea with Violet Wood.

'I'm amazed you weren't hurt when you fell off the bike. And you really should have told me first before going

off with someone you've just met! But
it sounds like you had a good time,'
Rose said more calmly. She flopped
down on to the sofa and patted the
seat next to her.

Lisa sat near to her aunt and Flame
curled up between them. 'John's really
nice when you get to know him, Aunt
Rose. He mended the buckled wheel.'
Oops. She hadn't meant to mention
that.

But Rose didn't seem to have
noticed. She sighed and put her arm
around Lisa's shoulder. 'No harm's
done. So let's forget it. But promise me
you'll always tell me where you're
going from now on.'

'I promise,' Lisa said, making a
cross-my-heart shape with one finger.

Rose smiled, her good humour
restored. She jumped up and went
towards the kitchen. 'Right, I don't
know about you, but I'm starving.
Could you bring the shopping inside,
please?'

'Um . . .' Lisa's face fell. 'Now I'm
really going to get roasted,' she
whispered to Flame.

Flame mewed and twitched his

whiskers. Lisa saw that huge silver
sparks were popping in the air around
him. The familiar warmth prickled
down her spine.

'Flame! You can't have . . . Can you?'

She dashed outside to where she had
left the bike leaning against the cottage
wall. The bike's basket was crammed
with food. There was bread, milk,
eggs and even a gooey, home-made
chocolate cake.

'Oh, you star!' Lisa swept Flame up in a huge hug. She kissed his pink nose. 'You've just saved my life!'

Flame widened his eyes. He stopped in mid-purr. 'Are you in danger, Lisa?'

'No. It's just something you say.' Lisa giggled.

Rose threw up her hands with delight when she saw the cake. 'That's my favourite!'

'My treat,' Lisa said, biting back a huge grin. She would have loved to say Flame chose it!

That evening after supper, Lisa washed the dishes without a second thought. She smiled to herself; she must be getting used to life in the countryside! Afterwards, she made a cup of coffee

for her aunt and took it through to the
sitting room. Flame was curled up
asleep on his blanket.

'Thanks. I could get used to this,'
Rose joked. 'So, what did you think of
Violet Wood?'

'She's great. I loved her cara– wagon,'
Lisa corrected herself. 'It was really small
inside, but with a wood stove and bed
and everything. Violet told us some
stories about her travelling days.'

'I expect it was a wonderful life,'
Rose said. 'It's a shame that some
things have to change so much. Violet
rules the Wood family with a rod of
iron – even the men! She really must
have taken to you. I've never heard of
anyone from the village being invited
to have tea with her.'

'Violet loved Flame too,' Lisa said.
'But not as much as I do.' She glanced
at the sleeping kitten, a warm glow
filling her chest.

Rose smiled. 'The Woods seem like a
really nice, friendly family.'

Lisa was glad her aunt approved of
John Wood and his family. 'Do you
know Mr Higgins? Violet didn't seem
to think much of him.'

Rose snorted. 'Robert Higgins isn't a nice man. You'd think twice about getting on his wrong side. He's jumped to the conclusion that the travellers have been poaching deer.'

'Violet said she told Mr Higgins that she was sure none of their men had been poaching deer, but he didn't believe her,' Lisa told her aunt. If Violet didn't think any of the Wood family had poached deer, then neither did Lisa.

She jumped up. 'I'll go and feed the animals and bed them down.' She tickled Flame gently to wake him up. 'Are you coming, Flame?'

Flame yawned and stretched. He purred eagerly and jumped down.

Rose stood up too. 'Thanks, love. I've

still got this patchwork quilt to finish. I lost a bit of time going off to look for someone who was late home,' she said with a twinkle in her eye.

In the barn, Lisa filled food dishes and water bottles and replaced soiled bedding. As she fed chopped carrots to the rabbits and guinea pigs, a thought came to her.

'Where did that magic food come from?' she asked Flame.

'I took it from the shop. Like you wanted,' Flame said. He frowned. 'Did I do wrong?'

'No. But I'd better go and pay for it. I've still got the shopping money in my pocket. We'll dash over and deliver it and I'll scribble a note to explain things.' Lisa grabbed her shoulder bag. 'Come on, Flame. Jump in. We'll only be a few minutes. There's no need to tell Rose.'

Lisa and Flame hurried across the green towards the line of shops. She pushed the envelope through the village store's letter box.

'Job done,' she said happily, patting Flame's soft fur. 'I really love having you here with me.'

'I like it too,' Flame purred contentedly from the opening of her shoulder bag.

The first stars glinted in the violet sky. A smudge of fading peach light just showed above the church spire.

'It's getting dark,' Lisa said worriedly. 'We'd better get back before Aunt

Rose finds out or she'll ground me for the rest of the holiday!'

She started jogging towards the cottage. There was a signpost beside a track she hadn't noticed before. It read 'To Lower Berry Road'.

'It must be a short cut. We'll go that way!'

On one side of the track there were open fields. Thick woods that were part of the estate Robert Higgins looked after stretched away on the other side.

Lisa had been walking for about five minutes when there was a loud bang.

'Oh!' she gasped, nearly jumping out of her skin. 'What was that?'

Flame reared up out of the shoulder

bag. The fur along his back stood on end. 'Danger!' he hissed.

Lisa's breath came faster. She saw beams of light moving through the trees. There were shouts and men moving towards her. More bangs broke the silence.

'They sound like gunshots,' Lisa said shakily. 'Come on, Flame. We're getting out of here!'

She clutched the shoulder bag in her arms so that she could run faster without jostling Flame about. She had taken a couple of steps when a dark-blue van drove up. It screeched to a halt, blocking Lisa's way. Lisa spotted the broken wing mirror.

'It's that van again!' she whispered to Flame.

The driver leaned out of the side window. He shouted to a man coming out of the trees. 'Who's that kid? Go and find out!'

Icy fear curdled Lisa's stomach. She couldn't move.

Chapter
★ EIGHT ★

A warm tingle spread over Lisa. She felt the sparks crackling in Flame's fur beneath her hand.

'You are safe,' Flame assured her softly.

A moment later a man dashed up to where Lisa was standing. He stared straight at her. 'What kid? There's no one here,' the man shouted to the van driver.

Lisa gave a shudder of relief. Flame had made her invisible!

'We must go now,' urged Flame.

Lisa didn't need telling twice. She ran past the van, where the driver was still frowning in puzzlement.

Five minutes later she emerged on to Berry Road. She could see her aunt's cottage. Running the last couple of metres, she slipped into the back garden and crept into the kitchen.

The sound of her aunt's sewing machine came from her workroom. Lisa stuck her head round the door. 'I'm going to my room now, Aunt Rose. I want to read for a while.'

Rose looked up with a smile. 'OK,
love. Thanks for seeing to the animals.
I'll look in on you before I go to
bed.'

Lisa heaved a sigh of relief as she
climbed the stairs. She had only just
about stopped trembling. What had
those men in the woods been doing?

Maybe they were shooting crows or
rabbits. They had seemed really angry
at being disturbed.

Thank goodness for Flame. Once
again he had saved her skin!

'Have you made any plans for today?'
Rose asked the following morning.
Sunshine set rainbow patterns dancing
from the crystal hanging in the
window.

Lisa told her she was meeting John.
'We're going fishing.'

'Are you taking Flame with you?'
asked Rose.

'You bet!' Lisa said. She wouldn't
dream of leaving him behind. Especially
after the way Flame had saved her last
night.

Flame wound himself round her legs affectionately.

Rose reached down to stroke him. 'Well, have fun, you two. Be back in plenty of time for supper, OK?'

'Definitely,' Lisa promised. 'Come on, Flame, jump in.' Looping her bag on to her shoulder, she set out for the White Hart.

John and Fly were already waiting when Lisa and Flame arrived. 'The river's this way,' John said. They went past the green to a line of silvery willow trees.

The river gleamed through the swaying branches. John led the way down a grassy bank. 'Our family's got special permission to fish here. Dad helps clear waterweed away in spring.'

Flame stretched out in the grass and closed his eyes, purring contentedly. Fly, who was cropping the sweet grass, swung his head round and gave Flame a friendly snort.

'I can't get over how much Fly likes that kitten,' said John, setting out his fishing things.

Lisa smiled. 'Flame's not just any old kitten. He's really special.'

John passed Lisa a fishing rod and a small, battered tin. 'You can use my spare rod. Do you think you can bait it yourself?'

'Sure! How hard can it be?' Lisa opened the tin. It was full of little, squirming white bodies. 'Ugh! Maggots!' she gasped.

John grinned. 'You nearly dropped the lot! What did you think was in there, breadcrumbs?'

'Something like that!' Lisa admitted, blushing. 'I don't think I can hook one of these on.'

'Give them here. It's dead easy. I'll do it for you.' John gave her the baited rod and showed Lisa how to cast the line into the river. Lisa soon had the hang of it and they settled down to wait for a bite.

The scent of warm grass drifted on the river breeze. A moorhen picked her way through the reeds.

'You've got a bite!' John suddenly declared. He reeled in the fish and slipped it into a net in the water. 'There you go. One fat brown trout.'

'This is fun!' Lisa said. She felt proud of catching her very first fish.

John beamed at her. 'You're not bad company for a girl *and* a townie!'

'Watch it! You . . . you road rogue!' Lisa laughed.

'Road . . . what?' John asked as he fell about laughing.

'Hello there! Caught anything yet?' called a voice. Mike Sanders came along the river path, a smile on his pleasant face.

'Not again,' John groaned, but he nodded politely.

Mike Sanders peered into the net. 'That's a fine supper for someone.'

'Yeah, it's Lisa's first ever fish,' John said.

Mike Sanders smiled at Lisa. 'Beginner's luck, eh?' His face suddenly turned more serious. 'Now, I don't suppose you've heard anything about a couple of deer that were killed last night, John?' he asked.

John shook his head. 'Why ask me?'

'Because I reckon you've got a level head on your shoulders. You'd know where to come if you got wind of anyone poaching round here, wouldn't you?' Sanders said.

John shrugged. 'Might do. But I don't know anything.'

'Where were they killed?' Lisa asked.

'In the woods near Lower Berry Road,' Sanders told her. 'Quite near

where your Aunt Rose lives.' He gave
John a friendly pat on the back. 'Well –
keep your eyes peeled, lad.' He looked
back before continuing down the river
path and called over his shoulder,
'Hope the fish keep biting.'

Lisa stared after him, her thoughts
whirling as she remembered the shots
in the woods last night and the men
with torches among the trees. Then
there was the blue van, which she had
seen twice now.

She had been tempted to tell Mike
Sanders her suspicions, but she hadn't
any proof. And she'd have to explain
what she'd been doing out near the
woods at night. That meant risking
getting into trouble again with Aunt
Rose.

Were those men the deer poachers? She pressed her lips together in determination. She and Flame were going to find out.

Chapter
* NINE *

Lisa stared out of the cottage window as drops streamed down the glass. It had been pelting with rain all afternoon. Aunt Rose was at the village hall running a workshop on making patchwork quilts. Lisa felt restless.

Flame jumped on to the window sill. He batted at the glass, trying to catch the raindrops. Lisa laughed and dangled a piece of wool for him to catch. 'You want to go out too, don't you? I hope it stops raining before tonight.'

Flame nodded and wrinkled his little pink nose. 'I do not like wet fur.'

Lisa planned to wait until dark and then go back up to the woods and have a good look around.

Just then she heard a knock at the kitchen door. It was John on Fly.

Lisa took one look at him. 'What's wrong?' she gasped.

John was soaked to the skin. His hair was plastered flat and his face looked pale and angry. 'It's my dad. He's been taken to the police station. They think he's been poaching deer,' John told her as he tethered Fly to the back porch. He looked like he might burst into tears.

'Oh, that's awful. I'm really sorry,' Lisa
sympathized. She fetched a towel so
John could dry himself.

John shoulders slumped as he sank
into a kitchen chair. 'It's Robert
Higgins's doing. I know it is. But I
don't get it. What's he got against my
dad? He's never done anything to him.'

Lisa bit her lip, wishing she could
think of some way to help. She got

him a piece of the delicious chocolate cake. 'Here you are.'

He cheered up a bit as he ate. 'Gran's furious, but she's dead worried too. If only there was something I could do.'

'Maybe there is,' Lisa said on impulse.

She told John about the gunfire and the men she'd seen in the woods. 'And I've seen that blue van twice. I know it was the same one because of the broken wing mirror.'

John jumped to his feet and paced round the kitchen. 'It must have been the poachers! Deer are big animals. You'd need a van to take them away. Maybe we should go and tell Mike Sanders.'

'I thought of that already. But we haven't any proof. Shouldn't we wait until we're sure about this?' Lisa reasoned.

John gnawed at his lip. 'You're right. And if the police start going round asking loads of questions, the poachers will go into hiding. That leaves my dad as chief suspect. But how do we get proof?'

'I've got an idea . . .' Lisa began telling him about her plan to go to the woods after dark.

John listened in silence, then a wide grin spread across his face. 'What time do we meet?'

'We?' Lisa grinned back. 'I hoped you might say that!'

'You don't think I'd let you have all the fun, do you?' John said. He got up and went towards the garden to untie Fly.

Lisa was relieved. It had been really scary up at those dark woods.

'All right,' she said. 'I'll meet you at midnight on the back path to the woods. Don't do anything before I get there, OK?'

'Who, me?' John flashed her one of his cheeky grins. He jumped up on to

Fly's back and urged the pony forward.
'See you tonight,' he called over his
shoulder.

The bedroom was dark except for the
digital display of her bedside clock.
Lisa jolted awake. Flame was licking
her chin. His whiskers tickled her
nose.

'Thanks for waking me!' She yawned
and rubbed her eyes.

'You are welcome,' Flame purred, his
fur twinkling in the darkness.

It was a quarter to midnight. No
time to waste. Lisa was fully clothed
beneath the duvet. Reaching for her
bag and a disposable camera, she and
Flame crept downstairs and out of the
house.

The moon sailed overhead, as bright
as a beacon. Lisa's eyes soon adjusted as
she made her way to the woods. Flame
trotted beside her. With his cat night
sight he moved as easily as in daylight.

'This is the path,' Lisa whispered,
pointing ahead. 'But look! The blue
van's parked near those bushes.'

Lisa's heart pounded as she and
Flame crept forward. She scanned the

path and clusters of trees, looking for John. But there was no sign of him.

Flame pricked up his ears. 'There are men in this wood.'

A moment later, Lisa heard voices shouting. 'Get him! He knows who we are!'

Shadowy shapes crashed through the trees. Someone shoved branches aside and rushed towards Lisa, gasping for breath. For an instant a slim, scared figure was caught in a beam of torchlight.

Lisa's eyes opened wide with shock. 'It's John!'

Chapter
★ TEN ★

Almost at once Lisa felt the familiar
tingly warmth down her spine. Silver
sparks crackled in Flame's fur and his
whiskers glittered in the dark.

'No one can see you, Lisa,' Flame
explained softly. He hung back, melting
into the deep shadows. 'Save John.'

Lisa let out a sigh of relief. Flame
had made her invisible again!

John stumbled out of a thicket right beside her. Leaning against a big oak he doubled over, clutching a stitch in his side. Lisa could hear the men coming closer. They would catch John at any moment. She had to distract them somehow.

Lisa started to run, her heart pounding. Her whole body began to tingle. A rush of heat swept through her. She felt her muscles bunch as she made a huge leap forward — and bounded along on all fours. Strong, tireless legs carried her on. Her hands and feet had become spread pads, which gripped the leaf litter with sharp claws.

She was a huge cat! A huge *invisible* cat!

Night smells flowed over her. The forest came alive. She could see every leaf and blade of grass and hear every tiny movement. The men seemed to move in slow motion. Their breath sounded like rushing water and their footsteps were as loud as drumbeats.

Lisa rushed up behind the first man and slammed into the back of his legs. He yelled with fright as his knees

buckled. In a swift movement, Lisa
changed direction and launched herself
at another man.

'Oof!' The second man fell sideways
into a clump of bracken.

'Grrr!' Lisa growled with triumph.
She tripped up the third man who
went over in a jumble of arms and
legs.

The three men picked themselves up. They looked round nervously. 'There's something weird in here!' one said.

Lisa grinned. She crept up close behind them and opened her mouth wide. 'Grrr-owl!!' she roared.

'What's that?'

'I don't know, but I'm out of here!' one of them cried. 'Get back to the van!'

Lisa knew that John was safe for the moment. Time to get the evidence they needed.

She bounded swiftly towards the parked van and reached it ahead of the men. The back door was ajar. Her cat senses caught the smell of death. Two deer lay in the back of the van. Lisa jumped inside, already fumbling for her camera. Her fingers closed around it.

Fingers? She wasn't a cat any more! Flame's spell must have worn off. Did that mean that the men could see her now?

There was no time to think. Aiming the camera, she took a photo of the dead deer. Suddenly, the back door was wrenched open behind her. But Lisa was ready. She stuck the camera in the men's faces. Flash! Flash! She took their photos.

'Wassat?' one yelled, covering his face with his hand.

'I can't see. I'm blinded,' moaned another, hopping about and bumping into his friends.

Lisa leapt out and dashed behind a tree. Moments later, the engine fired up and the van sped off up the track.

Lisa leaned against the tree and gave a nervous shaky laugh. Wow! That was close. She had loved being a cat! She couldn't wait to talk to Flame all about it.

She glanced around for him. Where was he? He usually kept close beside her. As she made her way back towards the track, she called softly, 'Flame. Where are you?'

'I am here,' came a tiny whimper. Flame crawled out from beneath some bracken. His eyes were wide with alarm.

Lisa picked him up. 'Oh, you're trembling.' She stroked his head and gave him a cuddle. 'Don't be scared for me. Your magic was brilliant! Those horrible men have gone now.'

But Flame nestled closer, his tiny heart beating fast. Lisa felt a stir of unease as he gave another little whimper.

Just then John ran up to her. 'Lisa? Where have you been? You've missed all the fun!' he panted. 'I know who the poachers are!'

Lisa gently tucked Flame into her shoulder bag. He would be warm and safe in there. 'Did you get a good look at them?' she asked.

John's face was white, except for a smudge of dirt on his cheek. He nodded. 'Two of them are friends of Higgins's! He must be in on it. No wonder he's trying to blame my dad. They tried to catch me, but I lost them in the woods.'

'I'm just glad you're safe,' Lisa said, relieved that they were both OK.

John frowned. 'I might be safe, but I still haven't got any proof. It's my word against theirs.'

Lisa felt in her pocket for the camera. She imagined the look on John's face when he found out she had taken photos. But her fingers closed on nothing but empty space.

Oh, no! The camera wasn't there. She must have dropped it in the woods!

'Photos? How did you get photos? You've only just got here, haven't you?' John frowned at Lisa in puzzlement when she had explained.

Lisa thought quickly. She couldn't let John know about Flame's magic. 'I saw

the blue van on my way to meet you.
No one was about. So I risked taking
some photos. But I nearly got caught
when they came back!'

John looked impressed. He whistled
through his teeth. 'Those photos will
prove my dad had nothing to do with
poaching deer. We really need to find
that camera. I'll look over where the
van was parked.'

'OK. I'll look over here.' Lisa went a
little way into the woods. Opening her
shoulder bag, she whispered to Flame,
'Can you help me find the camera,
please? I have to be getting back. Aunt
Rose will be furious if she finds out
I've sneaked out here at this time of
night!'

Flame was curled into a tight ball in

one corner. He lifted his head and gazed at her with fearful eyes. 'I must hide. My enemies are close. Uncle Ebony's spies are almost here,' he mewed.

'Oh, no!' Lisa's chest constricted. No wonder Flame was acting strangely. He was in terrible danger.

Chapter
ELEVEN

'You have to leave here, Flame! Now!'
Lisa urged in a shaky voice. Tears
pricked her eyes. The thought of her
friend leaving was heartbreaking. But
Flame's life was in danger and she
knew he must go.

Flame shook his head. His eyes were
dull and his fur was flat. 'I am too
weak. I need strong magic to find a

new place to hide soon. But not now,'
he told her in a small voice.

Lisa gulped back tears. She was
secretly relieved that they could be
together a little longer but she was still
worried for his safety. She stroked his
little velvety ears. 'Please be careful,
Flame. I couldn't bear it if they found
you.'

Turning his head, Flame touched the
tip of Lisa's index finger with his nose.
'You must find the camera.'

Lisa's finger felt warm and tingly and
the end began glowing softly. She
understood what she must do.

Flame's head drooped and he curled
back into a tight ball. Lisa saw with
dismay that only two or three little
silver sparkles glinted in his fur.

There was no time to waste. Lisa clutched her shoulder bag to her side and began searching for the camera, using her glowing finger as a guide. She scrabbled leaf mould aside and poked under fallen twigs. As she moved towards a tuft of grass, her finger stopped glowing. 'I must be getting cold.'

She turned back towards a group of
birch trees and her finger glowed
faintly. 'Now I'm hotter.'

She kept searching, watching for her
magic finger to give her clues. As she
stood over a thick clump of bracken, a
big spark shot right out of the end.
'Wow! I'm boiling now!'

Lisa pushed the fern aside. There was
the camera. 'Brilliant!' She scooped it
up and went to find John.

John was searching the long grass
beside the path. He straightened up
when he saw Lisa waving the camera at
him. 'You've got it? Great!' His teeth
flashed in a huge grin. 'Excellent! I'll
get the photos developed first thing
tomorrow morning. Gran will come
with me to see Mike Sanders. I should

like to see anyone argue with her, once they see the photos! Thanks a million, Lisa.'

Lisa blushed. 'Glad we could help.'

'We?' John said, looking a little confused.

'Me and Flame,' Lisa said.

'Oh, yeah!' John chuckled. 'Thanks, Flame. You'd better go now. Your aunt will skin me alive if she finds you out here with me!'

Lisa smiled and waved goodbye as she hurried back to her aunt's cottage.

She didn't see the long black shadows prowling through the trees. Two large black cats appeared for an instant. One of them lifted its head, scenting the air before they both disappeared.

There came a faint echo of a

powerful voice. 'The prince is near. We are close . . .'

Lisa crept in the back door and up through the darkened cottage.

'Phew, made it,' she breathed, closing her bedroom door behind her.

Now that the excitement was over, she felt really tired. She undressed and crawled into bed. Flame jumped up and settled down beside her. He reached forward and touched her chin gently with the tip of his cold, pink nose.

'You are a good friend, Lisa,' he said with a rumbling purr. 'I will never forget you.'

A hard ball of misery lodged in her chest and her eyes filled with tears, but she swallowed them bravely. 'Me too. I've loved having you here, Flame. But I know you have to leave soon.'

'Soon,' Flame agreed sadly and snuggled up under her chin.

Moments later, Lisa fell deeply asleep.

The next day, Lisa was in the barn. She was filling dishes with scoops of pet food and trying not to think about Flame leaving. She knew she should be feeling happier — she had heard from her aunt earlier that day that Higgins and his friends had been arrested. But she was just so sad at the thought of losing Flame. Right then he was sitting on the feed sack where she had first discovered him, his eyes watchful and intent. He kept lifting his head, testing the air for his enemies' scent.

Lisa had her arms full of hay when she heard her aunt calling. 'Lisa! You've got visitors!'

She looked up to see her aunt and two other people coming into the barn.

'Mum! Dad!' she cried with delight as she ran towards them and flung herself into their arms. 'What are you doing here?'

Mrs Morgan laughed. 'We missed you. So we came back early. Rose has asked us to stop for a few days before we all go back to London.' She turned to her sister with a smile.

'You don't mind, do you, love?' asked Mr Morgan, looking a bit worried. 'I know you've probably been really bored here in the country.'

Lisa realized that she had enjoyed herself far more than she ever thought possible. And this was mainly due to Flame. She was about to reply that she'd had a fantastic time when she noticed a flash of light from near the feed sack.

'Why don't you go into the kitchen?' she said hurriedly. 'I'll finish feeding the animals, then I'll come too.'

Rose led Lisa's parents out of the barn. 'Let's leave Lisa to it. She always insists on getting her chores finished by herself. She's been a great help to me.'

'Really? That doesn't sound like the grumpy girl we dropped off at the train station last week!' Lisa's dad said with surprise.

'She certainly looks a lot happier

than I expected!' said her mum,
looking slightly amazed. 'See you in a
minute, love,' she called over her
shoulder.

As soon as they had gone, Lisa spun
round. She ran towards the back of the
barn and stopped in her tracks, stunned
by what she saw.

An enormous young white lion
with glowing emerald eyes stood
there. His fur glittered and sparkled
and his whiskers glowed with light.
Prince Flame was no longer disguised
as a fluffy marmalade kitten. Beside
him stood an older-looking grey
lion, a calm expression on his wise
face.

As Lisa watched, silver sparks filled
the air. The two lions began to fade.

Prince Flame lifted his paw in a final wave. His mouth curved in a gentle smile.

'Be well. Be strong, Lisa,' he said in a deep growling purr.

Then he was gone.

Lisa stood there, a wave of deep sadness flowing over her. She wondered where Flame would go now to hide. Would he ever be safe from his uncle's spies? Would he one day rule his strange, magical land?

'Goodbye, Prince Flame,' Lisa whispered. 'Take care. Stay safe. I'll never forget you.'

She stood there for a moment longer, thinking of the wonderful adventure she and Flame had shared. Even though her heart was aching, she knew she wouldn't have changed a single moment.

At last she took a deep trembling breath. Her parents were waiting for her. She knew she would never tell them or anyone else about Flame. He would always be her very own magical secret. But there was still so much more to tell them. And she couldn't wait for them to meet John and Fly.

Magic Kitten

Classroom Chaos

Flame needs to find a purrfect new friend!

And that's how lonely Abi's time at boarding school becomes much more fun when a magical, fluffy black and white kitten appears . . .

A fluffy black and white kitten needs a friend!

Magic Kitten
Classroom Chaos

SUE BENTLEY

Magic Kitten

Star Dreams

Flame needs to find a purrfect new friend!

And that's how Jemma's biggest dreams become possible when a silky cream and brown kitten comes into her life . . .

A silky cream and brown kitten needs a friend!

Magic Kitten
Star Dreams

SUE BENTLEY

Magic Kitten

Double Trouble

Flame needs to find a purrfect new friend!

And that's how Kim manages to put up with her mean cousin when a fluffy silver tabby kitten comes to stay...

A sweet silver tabby kitten needs a friend!

Magic Kitten

Double Trouble

SUE BENTLEY

Win a Magic Kitten goody bag!

An urgent and secret message has been left for Flame
from his own world, where his evil uncle is
still hunting for him.

One word from the message can be found in a royal lion
crown hidden in each of the Magic Kitten books 1–4.
Find the hidden words and put them together to complete
the message. Send it in to us and each month we will
put every correct message in a draw and pick out one lucky
winner who will receive a purrfect Magic Kitten gift!

Send your secret message, name and address on a postcard to:
Magic Kitten Competition
Puffin Books
80 Strand
London WC2R 0RL

Hurry, Flame needs your help!

Good luck!

puffin.co.uk

Visit:
penguin.co.uk/static/cs/uk/0/competition/terms.html
for full terms and conditions

Magic Kitten

A Summer Spell
0–141–32014–1

Classroom Chaos
0–141–32015–X

Star Dreams
0–141–32016–8

Double Trouble
0–141–32017–6

puffin.co.uk

Coming Soon . . .

Moonlight Mischief
0–141–32153–9

A Circus Wish
0–141–32154–7

puffin.co.uk